I0777649

HOLDING ONTO HOPE

JODY KAYE

©2021 Jody Kaye

All Rights Reserved

No part of this publication can be reproduced, stored or transmitted in any form, or by any means (electronic, mechanical, photocopying, recording or otherwise) without the consent of the Author.

This is a work of fiction. Names, characters, places and incidents are a creation of the Author's imagination or are used fictitiously. Any resemblance to actual persons living or dead, establishments, events or locales is coincidental. Except the original material written by the Author, all books, songs, and product references are the property of the copyright holders.

This book contains adult language and scenes and is intended for mature audiences.

Cover & interior images: Shutterstock and Depositphotos

Cover Design & interior formatting: Jody Kaye

Special Edition Paperback

First Print: January 2024

www.JodyKaye.com

Splinter of Hope
Shred of Decency
Sliver of Truth
Holding Onto Hope
Home Wrecker
Deep Gap
Bleeding Heart
Shattered Soul

Holding onto hope that

it is never too late...

For Jessie

Chapter One

Kimber

"But are you living your best life?" I pose the question to Cece that's been on my mind as of late.

It's mill girls' day. A bunch of us are meeting up at our favorite boutique in downtown Brighton and getting coffee next door at Baked Beans afterward. Only Sloan, Cece, and I have shown up so far. The two of them have already sifted through half of Paisley's racks while Sloan plays the role of Cece's personal stylist, something she's well-suited to.

The sun is shining through the plate glass. As glad as I am to be hanging out with my best friends this morning, my eyes haven't adjusted to the light. Thank goodness no one cares I haven't taken off my dark sunglasses. I'm using my late shift at Sweet Caroline's and the drive back-and-forth to drop my son off with his pseudo grandparents for all it's worth. But, in my defense, I didn't roll my eyes when I asked Cece if she was happy.

I love Cees and her ambition to go after a career she was meant for. But she's been so focused she's forgotten to have fun. Cece is more than ten years younger than I am, and I don't want her to have the same regrets I do about the lost years before I met my husband, Trig. I wish I'd appreciated how easy life was when I had the chance, instead of stumbling over the roadblocks I'd put in my way.

With age, I've also come to know Cece won't understand my perspective for another decade. So, a bit of playful teasing that she has to dump the tub of vanilla ice cream she's currently in a serious relationship with is as far as I'm willing to push it.

Cece shrugs with a half-hearted and self-conscious smile as Sloan, my partner in crime, continues snagging clothes off the rack and putting them up to admire the colors against Cece's flawless skin.

It's a little unfair. I've got a stupid zit on my chin—the kind that's so far under the skin it hurts like a bitch—and a ton of concealer on to hide the redness. Aren't you supposed to outgrow acne?

Stupid hormones.

The store bell jangles. Holly, the assistant manager at Sweet Caroline's, makes a whirlwind entrance, allowing Cece to save face. She returns to the dressing room. I use it as an excuse to haul my behind back to the chaise and plant my lazy ass on its cozy cushions.

My to-go mug is resting on a side table and I take a sip, forgetting that it's decaffeinated swill. *Yuck.*

"What time did the boys hit the links?" Holly inquires.

"Too early, but it was intentional. Trig and I have plans later this afternoon and Jake is all about the nineteenth hole."

"Jake is all about any hole he can stick his putter into," Sloan mutters.

The three of us snort in unison.

"I don't care if we live in North Carolina, sane humans do not golf in January!" Cece pipes up from inside the dressing room stall.

I open a bleary eye and spy Holly twirling a countertop display.

"Will you bring me a pair of those silver dangle drop sets to see?"

"Sure thing." She hands me a card from the rack.

I brush my thumb against the intricate earrings and lift the tag, surprised it's got a slash with a markdown price.

"Gonna get it?"

"I think so." I sit and pull a bill from my wallet.

Paisley, the boutique owner and its namesake, scans and bags my purchase. I wave her off when Paisley offers me the receipt and coins. We shop here often and I'm currently using her store sofa as a bed. So give a penny, take a penny, right? Or a buck ninety-five. It all comes out in the wash. At Baked Beans, I tip Aidy when she makes my coffee, and she lives in my attic.

I walk back to the chaise and flop down like a moody teenager, staring at the ceiling while the other mill girls finish their shopping.

In the end, Cece has an armful of clothes to wear for her new job as a pediatric physician's assistant.

"You're not getting anything?" she asks.

I hold the tiny bag containing my earrings up by my index finger.

Holly's now futzing with bottles in a display of lotions. She twists the lid on a bottle and sniffs. "This smells pretty. And familiar. Hey, Cece, do you wear this?" Her nose wiggles, taking a second whiff.

Celine sidles up next to her. They stand around, inhaling each fruity, floral scent while Sloan is busy at the register.

I haven't had breakfast and my stomach rolls at the words, basil, watermelon, mint, and even strawberry. I'm moving past hungry to the point where my maudlin mood will be apparent if I don't start participating in the fun my girlfriends are having.

"What did you find?" I rise from the recliner and push my sunglasses above my brow, making them into a headband, but lean away from the icky perfumes. "Are we going to see Aidy?"

"Did your espresso kick in, dearest?" Holly counters the two swift questions with a pat on the arm.

"Yes, finally." I lie.

"How long until your next dose?"

Eight to ten hours, but who's counting? No one here. This hurts too much to share with my girlfriends.

"You're awful." I quip instead.

"Oh, I'm awful? Come here, let me hug you! Have you ever worked with *you* when you are caffeine-free? I'm terrorized by the idea of Owen becoming a big brother. Nine months of you drinking decaf at midnight and I'm jumping up and down when Jake drags his sorry ass into the club."

Holly's the first to pull out of the embrace, unaware my back has stiffened.

"Say what you mean, why don't you?" I stroke my long red hair back behind my shoulders.

We both snicker. I'm secure in the rapport we keep. But if Holly only knew.

"You know I will. I love you so much, I'll even buy your next grande."

There's only one thing I want more than a Baked Beans' grande. Yet, I'm done holding onto hope that this month will end any differently than the others have since my son was born. I'm sick and tired of feeling sick and tired for no damned good reason.

Sloan calls to me and I slide the sunglasses over my eyes again so none of them bear witness to the tears pricking behind my eyes.

Walking into Baked Beans, the smell of heaven assaults my senses. It's too bad perfumers don't make coffee scents like the candlemakers do. If the lotion we left Holly and Cece fawning over came in arabica or robusta I would have bought the lot.

Holly is right, this morning proves that un-caffeinated I'm not myself. However, I've been doing a fantastic job of pulling the wool over everyone's eyes for the past three months. I went cold-turkey when I got pregnant with Owen. Irritability combined with morning sickness didn't do me any favors, even though back then my day didn't start until dinnertime.

Sloan and I wait our turn at the counter. The same slice of heaven I felt inhaling the warm aroma of the coffee shop settles into my heart when the barista's face breaks into a wide grin. I can't stifle the smile I return. Seeing Aidy is like looking into a mirror at a youthful, and much happier, version of me. The other difference? Those violet highlights in her long red hair.

I gave Aidy up for adoption twenty-one years ago. It was the most selfless choice I've ever made, and also the most painful up until now. She is perfection all grown up, leading the life I dreamt for her, and blessedly untouched by the ugliness the direction my own life had taken when she was a child.

The moment Aidy stood up for her boyfriend, Morgan, letting her adoptive parents know she was capable of seeing past a person's flaws and accepting them for who they are, reinforced I'd made the best decision trusting the Fairley's to raise my daughter. She wouldn't have grown up with that level of confidence otherwise. I certainly didn't have it when I was her age.

Aside from the fact that Don and Ghillie Fairley have

stepped in to love my son, Owen, like he's their grandchild, the best thing about my relationship with Aidy is how close we've become. She and Morgan live on the third floor of my home. And for as busy as Aidy is with college and this part-time job at Baked Beans, it's rare—after close to nineteen years living without her—a day goes by that we're not able to spend more than a few minutes together.

We're like sisters and she's one of my best friends. Not many can say that about a child they've given birth to. When I think upon the reasons I decided to get clean and sober, this was an unimaginable reward. I'm grateful for the chance to witness the person she's becoming. Yet, that doesn't mean we share every secret, nor does it take away from the fact that Ghillie has been Aidy's mom since the day she was born.

"What'll it be, Sloan?" Aidy's already got her hand on the cup and cardboard sleeve, ready to lift the frothing pitcher to steam milk for my latte. "I already know Kimber's order."

"Actually, Dumplin', can I get one of those boba teas?"

"Chai? That's the one I brought home last week."

"Yes, please. And easy on the sugar."

"Coming up! Sloan?" Aidy puts away the shiny tools she was about to use.

"I'll stick with an Americano with soy milk, thanks."

My elbow pokes Sloan's rib. "You should have said 'weak bean water'."

It's what I've been choking down all morning.

"At least I'm saving my daily allotment of carbs for when it counts." She side-eyes me. "What gives with the no *coffee* for the *coffee* connoisseur at a *coffee* shop?"

"I had two today and am in the mood for something else. And I'm hungry, so the tapioca pearls will fill me up."

"So will a chocolate croissant, and the scratch-baked

ones here are worth every sinful calorie."

I make a *meh* sound. Although when Sloan adds one to her tab as we pay for our beverages, I secretly hope she'll let me tear off a flaky bite.

We leave Aidy behind the counter to do her job, knowing as soon as her break starts she'll join us.

Holly enters, places her order, and takes the chair opposite me and next to Sloan. She apologizes for being late, and then again for forgetting she wanted to buy my drink. It's not as if the opportunity won't present itself again. Holly's the type that gets to work in the nick of time and remembers important events as they're happening.

On the flip side, like most working moms, Holly juggles a lot, and she does it with the positive attitude of a cheerleader under the Friday night lights. Holly also rarely calls out sick, which makes her literally the best assistant manager anyone could ask for.

"What happened to Cece?" Sloan's brow furrows, and she glances at the entry. The line at the counter is getting longer.

"She said she didn't feel good and went back to the mill to sleep it off."

"Must be all those germy little people in the pediatric office."

"What do you have against kids all of a sudden?" Holly questions Sloan.

"Nothing. I like yours and hers." Sloan says about me. "I held O all the time when he was a new baby, didn't I, Kimber? My only point was she's around sick children, so I hope she's had her flu shot before any of them sneeze in her mouth."

Gross. However many times Owen's done that to me, my nose still wrinkles. My stomach tumbles at the idea. I need something more than tasteless decaf inside of it before it's too late and rethink my plan not to get a pastry or mini quiche.

In the nick of time, Aidy slides a tray with four drinks on it in front of us. She scoots her bottom onto the bench seat beside me and leans her elbows on the tabletop. "I switched breaks with someone else," she tells us.

I run my fingers through the trailing ends of purple in her long hair, thinking back to what Sloan mentioned about being enamored by a newborn O. Both of my babies were cue-ball bald. A familiar sharp pain stabs the center of my chest that's become increasingly difficult to ignore.

"Are you ready for the excitement this afternoon?" Aidy bubbles.

Sloan and Holly's expectant eyes land on me. My lungs fill with air and I puff out my cheeks.

Chapter Two

Trig

It isn't even noon and I'm nursing a beer on the nineteenth hole. I have better things to do today than stroke anyone's puny putter. In a perfect world, I'd be at home, sipping a second cup of coffee with my arm slung around Kimber, watching our kid play on the carpet with his toys.

I've got shit going on this afternoon that's more important than glad-handing a bunch of puffed up asses with their golf shirts tucked into their fucking pants. Wearing caps and jackets embroidered with either sporting company logos or their own business', these men are walking billboards. It's like the boomer version of Aidy's "look at me" social media feed.

Jake's in control of my morning, though. He wanted me to help him pull some strings, so he'd have the advantage on the back nine playing Rex Stanton. All I'd agree to was an early tee time so he could "accidentally" run into the man and strike up a conversation. With a Cheshire grin plastered on his ugly Nordic mug, Jake's across the room, chatting up Rex Stanton before the unsuspecting prick hits the links.

I sigh. My back teeth grinding.

Four friggin' hours on a Saturday stuck pretending I couldn't have outshot every pretentious man on the green this morning with one hand tied behind my back.

It's rare when Jake allows either of us a win. He needs them mailable to get what he wants, and that leaves me in the sand trap. Jake loves the hustle. Until the end, the friendly wagers build as they lose control of their over-inflated egos. Sometimes he ups the ante all the way to the end and then *poof!* he blows it.

Naturally, of course. There's a breeze that blows or a twinge in Jake's back and the ball sails in the wrong direction, quelling his lead. Or mine. I prefer making the rounds of the country clubs with Carver, who doesn't give a shit if I beat him because golf isn't Carver's snatch and grab.

I used to suck it up, enjoy the folly of fools, even. However, the number of times since Owen was born and Aidy came back into Kimber's life that I've wanted to tell Jake to take a hike are too numerous to mention.

Kimber and I have a good life. A house. A family.

Sure, like my wife, it's one I want to grow bigger, but that doesn't seem to be the hand we're dealt. Yet, nobody will ever hear me grumble that it's not enough. Kimber is more than I deserve and giving her one baby was a hurdle a few short years ago I wasn't sure we'd make it over.

Kimber was eighteen when she gave Aidy up for adoption and she struggled through those emotions and some heavy-duty postpartum depression without a support system.

Swigging down the last sip, I set my empty on the white linen table cloth. It's frou frou for a golf club's restaurant bar, but whatever. Twisting the bottle around, I stop myself from tearing at the label and shredding it into a pile.

I've made my fair share of messes. Jake? Today he's using that to his advantage.

Holly Carrington, the assistant manager at Sweet Caroline's, put in an application with the local big brother program for her son, Bhodi. The coordinator matched Holly's nine-year-old with a guy named Cary Cass. According to the information Cary gave Holly when they spoke, Cass is employed at a local car dealership. If his last name was Smith I doubt anyone would have thought twice. But cars across the Triangle have Cass-Stanton emblazoned upon their tailgates or holding the back license plates on.

Holly is a great mom. Every decision she makes is with that kid in mind. It was smart of her to come to me with a red flag. All she needed was for me to ensure she wasn't letting her kid go off unaccompanied with a deviant.

I didn't find a trace of drug abuse, a history of any arrests, or restraining orders. Cass keeps a low-profile online, has squeaky clean credit, a job with the benefit of eventually owning the damn company, and decent equity in a half-million-dollar house on the sound in Manteo. He drained his trust fund dry because of it. But if you ask me, the kid's not doing too bad. If Morgan wasn't shacking up with Aidy in my attic, I'd convince Kimber's daughter she was in the market for a new car.

Who knows why Cass is volunteering as a mentor? It could be as simple as It's part of his company's charitable outreach. However, it was a dumbass move on my part to mention to Jake I was looking into Cary Cass. Not only does my partner know the man already, Cary *Stanton* is also Rex's progeny. It drove Jake bonkers —not that it takes a hell of a lot—trying to piece together why the twenty-something dropped Stanton in favor of his grandfather's surname.

Of course, I've dug deep before for Jake Ballentine on other matters. One of Cass-Stanton's execs had certain proclivities that didn't include his wife and would have left a congregation of parents questioning if they'd misplaced their trust in the man who acted as a youth pastor to impressionable young men every Sunday. Sexual deviation is not tolerated in strict southern houses of worship.

Hell, I'd be more concerned about who was fucking the exec's wife if he was fucking someone else. But I also have a marriage of my own and a wife I haven't screwed around on since the moment I stuck my dick between her legs... And it isn't because I'm afraid a feisty redhead like Kimber would cut it off along with my balls.

She so totally fucking would.

But not Jake. He thought someone was off about Stanton and was correct figuring Rex would pay to keep his employee's secret. So, Jake hadn't bought it when I muddled through explaining the bad blood between Cary Cass and Rex Stanton was probably one generation trying to make its mark while the other wasn't ready to hand over control. I wanted Jake to leave it alone for Holly's sake. Admittedly, sleeping like crap has made me exhausted and I flubbed the shit out of it when I told him. Jake took advantage. Like a viper, he knows when to go in for the kill and the shithead gets worse year after year.

I thought Jake would settle down at some point. Start living his best life. Stop obsessing over, and falling for, women he can't have. And kick the worse habit of collecting and using all the ones easily attracted to him. Women can't change men unless or until the man finds the reason within to want to be changed. Even then, it's all on him.

At this point, I humor Jake because I know if he had his druthers Sweet Caroline's would have shuttered its doors when Jake's mother, the club's namesake, stopped stripping. Complying also gets me home in the company of the people who mean the most to me.

I adjust my ass in the chair and tap my fingers on the underside of the table. My bored expression attracts a waiter who asks if I want another round. I wave him off once and then again a few minutes later, saying no to the check.

In my peripheral vision, I'm able to see what's going on. Stanton's face is red and his fists are clenched. Jake's leaning in. His arm reaches high and his palm is flat to the wallpaper. He's placed his empty green beer bottle so close to a plant that it's practically inside. The cleaners will have a tough time noticing it. Stanton's puffing up. Jake's as cool as a cucumber.

I check my watch, giving it three minutes before Ballentine saunters back in a celebratory mood. He'll greet a member or two. Press the flesh. They'll fawn over him when he invites them to the club or suggests a tee time another day. They'll show at both places. They always do. He calls it respect, but let's not mince words. It's fear. Nobody here wants Jake to take an interest in their business, and they're senseless enough to believe if they're affable toward him, they'll stay on Jake's good side. These are men he controls or those who haven't realized someday he aims to have control over.

"You good?" Jake's all smiles, sitting down and scooting his chair in.

"You are," I quip, and his fangs show.

Jake'll brag about it once he makes himself comfortable and orders another round. He's in the mood for rum and makes the server go through all the top-shelf options.

I'm not drinking what he's asking for, so I don't give a shit when his brand isn't available. It's too close to the time I've got to head out to meet up with Byron Burne, and Byron will hit the fucking roof if he smells hard liquor on my breath before we get to work.

Jake tells the waiter nevermind and settles on the cheap stuff like I knew he would. The whole thing was a ploy to prove his dominance.

My friend is restless. He wants to spill, but I make Jake bite his tongue until his new drink is in front of him and the waiter is out of earshot.

"Did Stanton cop to it?"

"Nah, but from the way he was about to burst a blood vessel, there's no way the kid is his. Interesting enough," Jake taps by the corner of his eye, "Rex's fear makes me wonder if Cass is aware."

"What else could they have between them that made Cary take the grandfather's name?"

"You tell me."

I touch my beard. "Hell if I know. Guy's clean. Other than the number of women he's fucked." I flip my hand so my palm faces the air. "Still less than you have, so that can't be it. And he's definitely into chicks, so Holly's got nothing to worry about with Bhodi."

"What about Stanton? Any concerns about little boys there? Wouldn't be far-fetched with the people he employs."

"He's had a few work affairs with secretaries. None the wife seems to care about."

"And you're sure she knows?" Jake double-checks.

"Yeah, the past few years she's stuck close to the coast and lets Stanton do what he wants. Could be by mutual agreement."

"And there's no kid of Cass's they're keeping hush-hush?"

I roll my eyes, sick of the twenty-questions.

Sometimes it feels like being Jake's sleazy on-call private investigator is my lot in life. I'm whoring myself out for the guy and the pay sucks. My wife and I are damn close to being no more than his lackey's.

Amongst other things, I did surveillance in the Army. Carver backed my start-up when I got out. He gave me a place to live at the mill, and I met Kimber through the connection to Carver when she was one of Jake's dancers. The single thing I fucked up was taking a measly loan from Jake. One that I've repaid several times over, both monetarily and otherwise.

I'm getting too old for this. I think about calling it quits constantly. I've pocketed enough cash that I wouldn't have to work another day. And that's part of the issue, isn't it? I close up shop and don't even jaywalk during my remaining years and I'm still apt to take it up the ass if Jake, or Carver for that matter, get taken down.

What the hell is the point in redeeming myself if I can still go to jail for shit I've done in the past?

And then there's the fact that when Morgan fought his demons by defending Aidy against hers, his dumbass friend, Jasper, made an alliance with Mordecai. Jake's small-time in comparison to the operation Mordecai runs. He's a man you don't trifle with or expect to forgive your debt.

I don't know when Mordecai's going to call in his chips or if Jasper's debt will leave Kimber's daughter's boyfriend vulnerable. And the last thing I need is to go into retirement and find hell raining down on my family.

For better or worse, I'm stuck. There's too much at stake.

No fucking wonder I sleep like crap and am plagued with nightmares.

"I'm out." I say, standing up.

Too bad it doesn't have the meaning behind it I'd like

to have.

Chapter Three

Trig

There's a storm rolling through Brighton. It's raining steadily on this side of town. The wind blows and the heavy door whacks me in the backside as I enter the modern barn. Disinfectant veils the scent of animals. Not one-hundred percent. Even if it weren't for the barking down the corridor, it's still obvious there are dogs here.

The slam behind me attracts Tallulah's attention. She and Jovie are several strides across the linoleum. Jovie sits and says. Tallulah leaves the bone she's been chewing and scampers over to me.

I chuckle at the way her floppy ears bounce with excitement. They fold in long triangles down the sides of her face, touching her collar. When she was little, I joked around with Byron, wondering aloud if she'd grow into them or if Tallulah would be more like a goofy basset hound pup. She was continually tripping over her paws, skidding to a halt, or tumbling over. That's any puppy for you, though.

I squat down, giving her chin a scratch. "Miss me, girl?" I ask before standing and adjusting my slacks.

Tallulah takes my left flank, sits, and looks up, waiting to obey my first command. I tell her she's a good dog while stuffing my toque in my back pocket.

"She knows you!" Byron claps. "I was going to redirect her, but wanted to see what she'd do." Burne, my former Army buddy shakes my hand. He motions to the clothes I wore golfing. "Aren't you looking smart on graduation day?"

I shrug it off. "No time to change. I would have worn my dress blues."

Byron chuckles, slapping me on the back. "Y'all ready to bring her home to momma?"

My therapist suggested an emotional support animal may help me, and Kimber and I made the decision to get one almost a year ago. We timed the wait, wanting Owen to be the slightest bit older and trying to find the best dog.

I mentioned it to Byron in passing, who jumped on the idea. If there's anyone I trust to know what they're doing, it's him.

When we served together, Byron was the soldier who went gooey-gooey for every roadside stray. He grew up a farm boy, surrounded by roaming animals. There's not one he can't find affection for. I swear he would have turned our Humvee into a third-world taxi service for any desert dogs we pulled up alongside.

That's how he got Jovie. The dude literally rescued her as an emaciated foundling at the end of our last tour, then jumped through hoops to get her on US soil. The local paper did a feel-good write-up about it, which caught the attention of a non-profit that connects service dogs with vets. After separating, Byron went to work for them training dogs and he now also coaches new handlers through a vigorous program.

No different from any other vet, I didn't get a say about Talulah. I'm Byron's *pet* project. Byron matched Tallulah to my needs based on what he knew about my personality after we were bunkmates overseas. Having actually been with me during most of the worst incidents, Byron has a keen understanding of what my nightmares are like. Or at least, what they used to be like.

Byron had them too. But back then, our minds were convinced our patrol was under attack and, as the years go by, mine is telling me I can't shield my loved ones from the heat and flames trying to outrun a blast. The more stress I add to my plate, the worse they get

Bad dreams were an infrequent but still a normal occurrence before Kimber and I got married. She was used to the marks I left on her when I'd lash out or grab her in the middle of the night. She accepted the risk of sleeping in my bed and went as far as to cover up her bruises. Never out of shame for being abused, but to protect me from the torment I felt when I saw I'd hurt her. My wife's burden weighs heavily on me, and it keeps the cycle going. Internalizing my misery for the unconscious abuse when all I wanted to be was her protector, the dreams rage on, making the situation worse.

I trusted Byron with my life overseas. He was a former confidant I'd lost touch with until a short while ago. During the few hours I've spent with him and the dogs on weekends, I've opened up about shit that's bugging me the same way I'd done when Byron and I were deployed. Although, so far, I haven't acknowledged the work I do for Jake. That's taught me the fine art of silence. Keeping your trap shut is better than giving anyone ammunition against you or accidentally dragging someone decent down a dirt road they shouldn't be traveling.

I'm not sure I belong on this path either. But I made the choice to join my friends before Kimber and my marriage were ever a glimmer. Carver, Jake, and I were a bunch of angry guys, who decided to use the world to our advantage the way we felt as we'd been taken advantage of. Consequences be damned. Years later, I'm a man who realizes he's cursed himself and there's no turning back the clock.

With Tallulah obviously ready to work, Byron puts us through our final paces here at the facility. My support animal may not need the over-the-top coaching, but I appreciate she's been raised alongside the best. Tallulah is a year old and Byron found her through an owner who was about to surrender her to the animal shelter when she was only a few months. He encouraged Kimber and me to come meet her and, once we had my wife's seal of approval, Byron took her in. I'd thought we were taking her home right away, but he's strict with his dogs and her training… And mine.

Every weekend I show up and Byron teaches me what I need to know so my pup and I can get along. Afterward, we play out in the fenced field. Tallulah and Jovie chase balls and blow off steam. I feed her treats and we bond. Lately, leaving her when the session is over is akin to when I leave Owen. This dog keeps taking little pieces of my heart, and I'm glad to finally be bringing her home.

"How have things been?" Byron asks, pitching a stick for Jovie.

The storm has passed. We're outside. Tallulah is galloping back toward me, her mouth around a ball she's fetched. She stops by a mud puddle, drops it, and sniffs. I drag her attention back to me with a whistle and happily she forgets and trots back the rest of the way with her toy.

"Wish O were as easy to distract," I josh. "He'd have been knee deep in that."

"You lucked out this time since she's playing. I can only train so much instinct out of her." Byron goes on with an affable warning, "Talulah is a hound. Plots were bred to work in a group to bring down large animals like bears. It's in her nature to hunt. You have to maintain control. She has to stay on a leash when you're out and about or she's going to take off on you when you least expect it. Dogs are dogs. Even the best ones will surprise a person and nip. Even the most obedient have minds of their own and will act on impulse. You respect her and she'll be inclined to do the same, keep following your lead, and want to please you. Be the alpha and she'll fall into line."

"Should I worry about her with O?" We don't have sentimental pictures of me sleeping with our newborn on my chest. I was too fearful of what might happen if I jerked. I won't even lie down in my son's bed now if he's sick or tired. We snuggle upright and in a chair to read books.

I understand the last thing any parent wants is their kid getting hurt, but it's my mental health that causes the problem in my home. In good conscience, I can't sleep next to my child, and I can't be bringing in an animal to help me with my issues that'll be a danger to Owen.

"Would you leave your kid unsupervised with someone you don't know?"

"I wouldn't leave him with some people I do know."

"There's your answer. Owen and Tallulah are going to grow up together. But they still need time to get comfortable with each other… You didn't answer my question, by the way."

"What question was that?"

"Asshole." Byron's conscious I'm avoiding and doesn't hold back.

"Jerkface," I grouse. "Things are ok. Not great." I won't lie. "Kimber's frustrated. I am too. Who knew after trying so hard not to accidentally knock the wrong woman up, it would be hard to do a second time with the right one? I think she's close to throwing in the towel." It's hard for me to ignore the bitterness in my voice.

"It's not you or her." Byron knows we went through a battery of tests when Kimber started taking fertility drugs. "So what is it?"

"Beats me. Bad timing?" I would have waited forever for my wife to be ready to have our son. Yet in my worst moments—when Kimber is devastated and I can't fix it for her—I wonder if I should have pushed her to start trying to have a baby before Aidy turned eighteen.

Retrospect has me analyzing every move I've made. I've gone as far as making deals with a God I half-heartedly believe in. I've compromised with the devil enough times. I'm running out of options other than to pray there's something bigger out there that can heal this gaping wound she's carrying.

Stupid me, I thought falling for our baby boy and watching him be carried about the house by his older sister would be the salve to heal every heartbreak. I hadn't expected watching the babies Kimber gave birth to bond would agitate the bruising and leave us with a new form of grief.

It's not just her sadness that's putting us through the wringer. It's the sum of the parts. I want another kid for her, and I want one for me.

Between baby stress and Jake bullshit, I'm punchier than ever. If something doesn't give soon, I'm going to need to start sleeping on the couch because of the flailing I do at night.

"For a single guy, your interest in my wife's nether regions is concerning."

I may be balking, but I'm also the one who opened up about this to Byron. He's not overstepping. Besides my wife and her doctor, there's no one else to talk to about it. Even if my friend doesn't have the first clue what we're dealing with, I appreciate his concern.

Byron opens his mouth, chawing a piece of gum he's been chomping between his molars since we grabbed our hats and jackets. "Man, your wife is hot. Doubt I'm the only one wondering. All I'm saying is if this isn't a job you're up for, I'm glad to stand in for you."

He chuckles and I growl.

Byron shoves my shoulder. "Relax, fucker."

"Nobody else is wondering, and I'm pretty sure that's the worst advice I've heard," I mutter. Then I call my dog and pull Tallulah's leash from my back pocket.

Byron still has a snarky look on his face. It's the one that he used when we were bunkmates and I was bullshit over whatever was going awry and, same as always, it's telling me to chill out. This too shall pass, and my hard focus on it is making matters worse. Byron is the only man on this earth who knows me as well as Carver and Jake.

Poor sap.

We harness the dogs and Byron follows me out to my vehicle, un-offended by my lame exit. The roles have been reversed and his grumpy ass has ditched me on several occasions.

I stand there for a second, searching for a way to say thank you for putting up with me and for all the effort he's put in with Tallulah. In the end, I say just that and we shake.

It feels a little like the goodbye we gave one another after our last deployment when we'd spent a year knocking each other down a peg with stupid wisecracks and building each other up when the outlook was bleak.

"One o'clock Saturday," he reminds me we have a check-in scheduled and need to be back at the barn. "If there're any issues call."

I hide my grin. "There won't be. I'll see you next week. Now that we're done the hard work, I may bring beer."

"You do that," Byron claps me on the back, "and reporting in on your progress may become an every weekend thing."

Chapter Four

Kimber

"Oh! You're home!" I gush, tossing the rag to the side that I've been using to wipe the kitchen counter off with, and dashing to the front door.

Trig's just come in with Tallulah. Today is so important for my husband and I want him to know that if this dog is going to help his anxiety and the depression he deals with after a nightmare, then she's a welcome addition.

At this point, she may be the only new member of our family.

Tail wagging, Tallulah strains on her short tether. She gives Trig puppy dog eyes to be let off-leash and play.

"Sit," he tells her, and her butt plops down on command. The tail keeps jiggling. It melts my overly hormonal heart.

I kneel down and stroke Talulah's head. Her floppy ears are like silk. I bring my palm under her soft chin, admiring her silky, brindled coat. "You've grown so much. Yes, you have." I baby-talk to her.

Tallulah licks her chops, her tongue a fraction of an inch from sliding against my cheek. It's adorable, and admirable how she's holding back. Byron has done an impeccable job with her. I thought we were getting a random puppy to housebreak. Come to find out he's provided us with as close to a full-fledged service dog as we could ever find.

I'm actually glad Aidy brought up at Baked Beans the fact that Tallulah was joining us today. With so many thoughts running through my head, I'd kept her mostly a secret. The mill girls aren't dumb, I've never hidden that Trig and I haven't been *preventing* since I gave birth to O. Yet I also haven't told any of them how hard we're struggling to have a second baby. Risking sharing our excitement about Tallulah seemed a good way to have that backfire on us too.

As soon as Aidy let the cat out of the bag, the girls were peppering me with twenty questions. Their elation had mine bubbling to the surface. Since I got home with Owen, I've washed Tallulah's bowls and made sure she has fresh water, arranged her dog beds both upstairs and down, and taken the tags off of the toys we bought for her.

Trig cocks his chin, his eyes narrow at me dancing with mirth. "Glad the dog is figuring out the pecking order around here, My Love." My jovial husband interrupts.

I stop fawning over the bundle of fur and stand, pressing my lips to his. "Welcome home to you too, handsome."

"Thanks." He snags my chin between his thumb and forefinger, kissing me a second time for good measure. I cup his cheek, caressing the trimmed hair of the beard he's growing back out after a short-stint clean-shaven. I liked our son's reaction to seeing Trig's face for the first time. But I missed this Trig too.

I miss the years when I used to lie in his arms in his room when we lived at the mill and believed our problems had any significance. The reality is those were our golden years—after Trig was out of the military and I'd kicked my addictions—and the only bad things that were happening to us were hardships we brought on ourselves. Now misery arrives uninvited at our doorstep.

Awake or asleep, I feel the way Trig's body tenses as he jerks during the night. And I worry I add to the agony he's dealing with because of my own despair. I'm not getting any younger and we're running out of time trying to have another baby.

In my darkest moments, I wonder if the saying is true that you should be careful what you wish for. All I wanted for nearly twenty years was another chance. A real opportunity to be a mom. To watch my baby grow and thrive the way I'd lost out on with Aidy. Safe, and warm, and loved by her parents, it was still a feeling that haunted me while my daughter grew up before my eyes in snapshots Ghillie and Don sent to me. I hadn't realized until I saw Trig holding a tiny blue bundle that we'd made together in his massive arms how overwhelming the sensation would be to have more children.

I frown and Trig pretends not to notice, kissing the furrow in my brow. He's aware of where my mind has gone. These conversations stay in our bedroom, behind closed doors.

"Where's O?" he asks, unsnapping Tallulah so she can sniff and roam.

"Outside on the swings with Morgan. He found all the squeaky toys and was laying in the dog bed pretending. The noise was a little much and something I thought maybe we needed to nip in the bud before he was playing tug of war with his teeth and lost a tooth on a rope."

"Good call." My husband's chest rumbles. His hand encircles my waist and I pop his favorite knit cap off his head. Static crackles, standing his hair on edge.

"How was your game this morning?"

"Horrible." He shakes his head.

There's no way.

"You love golfing."

"I love *winning* at golf and I can't play a fair game when Jake's…"

"Being Jake?" I finish for him. I love my boss in that platonic, I'd-be-devastated-if-anything-caused-his-demise sort of way. However, I've also known Jake long enough to realize he is the most likely candidate to cause his own downfall. Trig didn't like me at Sweet Caroline's during daylight hours, but he never barricaded the entrance either.

I smooth my hand over his chest, patting down his biceps.

"Go another day. Ask Carver to play a round. Take Morgan. Take Byron as a thank you. Don't give up on something you love because Jake's made it an obligation you can't stand… Just don't include him."

"Easier said than done."

"Say no next time. Use me as an excuse. Jake won't fight you about me."

"The man really needs his own wife to run his bar instead of mine."

"Fat chance of that. Hell would freeze over before Jake ever fires me. He can't stand the club. I'd have to quit first." I smirk. "Enough of the shop-talk. Come on. There's an excited little boy waiting outside to show *his* new dog *his* big backyard."

It's brisk and damp, but we spend most of the afternoon outside. Owen and Tallulah take turns chasing one another around the yard. Both have their tongues hanging out of their mouths. They collide a time or two and Owen rolls on the grass. The dog pokes her wet nose to his cold, red cheeks, enticing giggles from my toddler. Trig redirects her when she gets too playful for his liking, and I'm impressed with how easy Tallulah takes to his commands.

Aidy comes home from her shift at Baked Beans while Morgan is showing Owen the finer points of fetch. She's been teaching Owen how to pitch softballs, and my son tells my daughter's boyfriend he's throwing wrong. While trying to fix his stance, Owen mispronounces Morgan, dropping the g.

The three adults snicker.

"He's going to grow out of that, right?" Morgan asks.

"I don't know, *Moron,*" she says. Aidy thinks it's adorable.

There was a change in my daughter I couldn't quite understand after her Freshman year at Pinewood. She was sullen, but that's also when she began dying her hair that beautiful shade of lilac. There were a few months where my concern grew. It seemed like she was avoiding her mom and dad. Around the same time, she began dating Morgan, and bit by bit my beautiful girl came around. Her confidence has grown as she's fallen more and more in love with him. I like watching their reliance on one another and seeing them interact; sometimes as the cute young adults and others when they pretend to be entrenched in the seriousness of an old married couple. It's nowhere close to the type of relationship I had at her age. Aidy's biological father left me when he discovered I was expecting. I'm so glad she's found someone who makes her happy.

The sun sets early and we head inside. Tuckered out, Tallulah finds her bed in the living room. Morgan and Aidy go up to the attic to make a quick change. They're meeting Jasper and Hailey at the mill in an hour. Trig tries to entertain O while I start dinner. He fusses and cries, banging on the gate, trapping him downstairs, and bellowing for his sister.

I swallow hard. My knuckle wipes at my eyes. I nearly cut my nose off with the knife I hold in my hand to chop an onion with. Thankfully, Owen's tantrum drowns out the sound of my sniffing.

He's a sucker for his big sister and lucky that Morgan and Aidy care for him the way they do. In essence, he's their practice kid. Though my daughter could have made me a grandmother a few times over already, from what I've gleaned, the couple is waiting to take the rest of the steps in a traditional order. I've pondered if I'm being impatient about a baby. I'm not jealous of Aidy. Along with every person under this roof, she means the absolute world to me. But if Owen wants her, is what he really wants a younger, more energetic mom?

I manage a lot of young women at Sweet Caroline's. I connect with them and their interests and hadn't considered myself old until I saw "advanced maternal age" scribbled on my chart when I was pregnant with O. The abbreviation mocks me now.

Any children Aidy and Morgan have won't be too far off in years from the baby I've had with Trig. Am I too old to be raising more children alongside my daughter? Or am I supposed to be showering a grandchild with the attention I want to give my own baby?

Maybe this is why nothing has worked so far. I've thought every *why-not?* scenario through a dozen times. This one is nothing new.

My husband gives up on our toddler and sits down on the couch. Tallulah decides she'll snuggle him and hops up beside Trig, curling into the cushion with her head on his lap. He strokes her head and leans his neck back, trying to relax.

Good girl. I think. She's here for when Trig needs her. This afternoon was great. But I'm sure the morning's events haven't been cast aside in his mind. Underneath an exterior that screams he doesn't have a care, my husband's trouble is he cares so deeply.

I'm plating the skillet dinner that is coming off the stove when Aidy and Morgan come back downstairs.

"Donne-go-ho-ho!" Owen wails.

Aidy picks him up, and he tucks his head to her neck. Morgan rubs his back.

"We can stay?" She offers.

"No, Dumplin'. He's exhausted from all the excitement and you worked all day. Go enjoy yourselves."

My toddler is predictable. As soon as he's buckled into his high chair and stuffs a fistful of dinner in his mouth, he grabs for his milk. His lids drift closed while Trig and I exchange blithe glances. Owen's gone from the terrible twos to endearing in minutes.

Crying over, we eat in blessed silence and talk about all the times Owen has fallen asleep at the table, the way we knew he'd do tonight, and the wonderful moments we've spent with our little boy so far.

"I'll put him to bed," Trig says, taking our empty plates to the sink.

"No. I want to. Feed Tallulah. She must be starved, and she did a great job waiting in the other room while our food was out. I'll meet you upstairs after you've let her out."

I move the tray and unbuckle a floppy O, cradling him to my chest. He's perfect even when he's a hot mess. Holly's assured me that two won't last forever. And with my son's birthday around the corner, I'm a little afraid of how right she is.

Chapter Five

Kimber

There are precious few corny mom activities I enjoy more than tucking Owen in on the evenings I don't work. We converted his crib into a big boy bed and, after his tub, I can now snuggle my body around his while we read. Running my fingertips through my son's sweaty red locks and kissing his temple, I realize tonight's bath will have to wait until the morning.

I stare in awe at the most precious gift Trig's given me besides his patience and wondering how Tallulah will fit into O's bedtime routine on Daddy's nights in charge. Owen is lucky to have a father who participates. I'd love to be a fly on the wall to see what transpires between a man and dog—that his son is amusingly convinced belongs to him—and that little boy.

I don't need to manage Jake's club. I do it because it's something I'm good at. The hustle of activity serving customers from behind the bar allows me to forget my failings. The drama in the dressing room reminds me others have problems too: Aches and bruises that are no more or less than I've endured and struggles that are as important in their lives as the ones washing to the surface in my own.

Secretly, I've considered leaving and being "just a mom". I think just being an anything is probably the most important title any person can describe themselves as having because nine times out of ten I've found there's a level of selflessness to it. As much as I don't want to miss out on anything with Owen, it's my experience without my daughter that stops me. Those years seemed to drag, but looking back they went oh-so-fast. I keep working because it is selfish. My son will be grown and then who do I take care of? Who am I? And where will I be?

And also, who will be here? There's a distinct possibility of my husband serving time.

I've been to the club when it is closed. Bloodsuckers and the undead do walk in daylight. I'm not so blind as to why Jake seeks out Trig's help. I simply keep my nose clean when it comes to their business dealings. Pretty comical for the amount of blow that once streamed through my veins.

I ponder all the testing Trig and I've passed with flying colors and what my specialist has said as I enter the master bedroom. Walking straight to the mini-fridge that hides all of my medications, I gather the supplies I need. I have no tubal abnormalities. I got pregnant lickety-split when Trig and I decided to have a baby together. Other than my age, there's no glaring reason for my secondary infertility. I'm the healthiest I've ever been—minus the mental state that being unable to conceive puts me in. I'm never sure how finite the moments of happiness are.

In the bathroom, I rip open an alcohol prep pad and wipe it over my skin. In the hallway, I hear Trig's boots on the stairs and the jangle of Tallulah's collar. He must be letting her investigate the second floor and I use the time to my advantage. Flicking the air from the syringe, I jab the needle into my stomach. My soul finches, but I never do. The first time I hesitated shooting up was the last. Memories of my former addictions overwhelm the contentment I felt carrying my son in my arms to his room. I wish this shot ended in a euphoric high. Like my personal problems with alcohol, the devotion the junkie who lives within me has for the way the tip pricks my flesh is dangerous. I don't have the mental fortitude to do this much longer.

Trig spies the empty syringe lying by the sink. His brow creases and I can't meet his gaze. We know what was inside the vial. Yet, he's aware I'm at my tipping point and he's struggling to stop my fall.

Pushing past where Trig stands in the threshold, I break my silence and say the words that have been on the tip of my tongue for months. They're ones I don't want to admit. "This is the last time. I can't do it anymore."

The emotions going through this are all-consuming. They threaten the life we've already created, Owen, and tear at the foundations of our marriage.

My vision hazes and I hide my face in my palms so Trig can't see the tears streaming down. I'm a failure for conceding defeat. But the inability to get pregnant has made me feel like one anyway. I thought voicing this was the end would stop the hard truth from eating me alive. But it eviscerates me. The grief in my chest is a pain I haven't endured since I handed my first baby to someone else to raise.

The stark difference? Ghillie was exactly what my real child needed and this sends my imaginary baby to purgatory where they're abused by a demon and subjugated in despair. Nonetheless, I'm grieving the loss of faith.

Trig's steady palms encase my shaking shoulders. He spins me around, moving my hands and cradling me to his chest. His cheek rests on the top of my head. His shirt dampens from my heaving sobs. I have the sensation he'd cleave himself in two and pull me all the way into his body if that kind of magic were at all possible.

Tallulah enters our bedroom, forcing her nose between us. Still holding on, Trig guides me to sit on our bed. His dog rests her chin on my knee. I pat her head so that I won't scare her into thinking I'm the worst dog parent in the universe. A mangled laugh chokes from my throat and I continue crying, using the broadest shoulder I have to lean on. Guilt settles in. No wonder why my husband needs an emotional support animal. I add to his stress by asking for comfort.

Trig plays with Tallulah's ears, running them between his fingertips. Reassuring her she's right where she belongs. He consoles me with assurances that seek to mend my broken soul. Showing through his actions and his words that while right now I may not believe I'm enough for me, I will always be enough for him.

"Tell me where you are with all of this, My Love, so I can be there with you."

"I'm almost forty years old. Maybe I'm not supposed to have any more kids."

"You've held onto hope for this long." He counters as if to ask what's unfurled my grip from the fraying rope.

"What if I've already gotten everything I deserve?"

"I don't think that's possible, My Love."

I grow impatient, angrily wiping the wetness from my face. "Could you hear me out before trying to shove rays of sunshine up my ass and saying you'll give me the world?"

"Okay." He removes his arm from my shoulder. "Explain."

"What if you, O, and Aidy are supposed to be it for me? Having the three of you is far more than I'd expected when my life was a mess. Maybe you're the people I'm supposed to cherish above all else? Maybe being clean and sober was the reward and having this family was the cherry on top? Why am I trying to push it? Think of all the things that could go wrong."

I was considered advanced maternal age when I had Owen. Any pregnancy at this juncture is high-risk as are the chances of abnormalities. I gave up one child so they had a chance at a better life. That's my peak of selflessness. I can't lose another child. I won't have the strength to make any choice other than to carry to term. And where my mind has painted a bleak picture of never conceiving again, all I can see is the further strain it would put on my marriage.

"Think of all the things that can go right." He laces his fingers into mine.

"So you don't think we're finished?"

"If you're done. I'll be done. If you don't want the risks having another baby brings, I can abide by that choice. If you're worried about how long it's taking, there's adoption."

"That can take years too. A home study could very well put us out of the running."

"I can talk to Marie Grant, the woman who handled Hailey's guardianship with Carver."

"I can't do this the wrong way by bending the rules, Trig. Not when it comes to an innocent child."

His lips flatten to a line. "I know you can't. It's one of the reasons I love you. I just want to fix it, and I don't know how else to patch the hole in your heart." He sighs and his eyes water. "It was so easy giving you O and hoping it would fix all the hurt. And I love Aidy. The longer she's been under our roof, the more I feel like because she's a part of you, she's mine. I can live with that. What I can't live without is you."

I nod, mouthing "okay" back in a less than convincing manner.

Trig drags me up the mattress to settle our head on the pillows. We lie on our sides, spooning. Tallulah jumps up, taking my side of the bed. She curls herself against my belly, keeping me warm.

"I've wanted no one but you since the day I saw you." Trig reminds me in a hushed tone as exhaustion causes us to drift off. "You've always been enough. The one person I was searching for. My Love. I will do anything for you." His voice cracks, growing hoarse. "Anything."

Somewhere in the night Tallulah gets up. I hear her paws on the hardwood outside our door and have a vague awareness of the silence when she returns. I'm about to nudge Trig to see if she needs to go out when the dog winds herself in circles and lays down on a plush bed identical to the one in the living room.

My sleep broken, I glance at the image of my sleeping child on the video monitor. Then I get up and use the bathroom. The seam of my jeans has cut an imprint into my legs. I toss them to the hamper and tip-toe back in my t-shirt to slide between the sheets, finding Trig has done the same in my absence.

His front finds my back and his arm stretches over my thigh, caressing its way up to my breast and back down my stomach. Skimming his fingertips underneath the elastic of my panties, I clench my eyes shut, imaging us back at the mill and the pleasure Trig enticed from my body.

We twist. His boxers get shoved down somewhere in the blankets. My panties too. My husband hovers over me and I dare a peek at the sleepy softness in his expression and the concentration he has when he enters me.

Trig tucks his nose to my neck, rocking into my pelvis. His tongue traces my jaw and he kisses me with the same hesitancy and vigor he had for our very first kiss.

A few hours ago, I couldn't have bared his hands on my body. The mechanics of sex. The timing of his release. The incessant thoughts that *this could be it* that plagued my mind.

Tomorrow I'll have regrets over my breakdown. I'll second guess my decision to stop trying to get pregnant. But tonight I allow myself to forget for a moment about sperm counts and ovulation and timing intercourse based on the refrigerator filled with synthetic hormones with side effects that make me the weepy, worst version of the woman I want to be for everyone I care about.

I feel cherished. My body is not a vessel in waiting, but alive with its own seductive heartbeat capable of fulfillment.

Trig coaxes me to the brink, conscious of each sound I make and the telltale pull of my physical responses to the push and pull of our hips. His orgasm follows mine, thrusting deep within me. He stills, staying between my legs and resting like a shield over me.

Chapter Six

Trig

One of the fucking stupidest things I think I've ever heard—that on second thought makes a hell of a lot of sense—is when Kimber's fertility specialist told me I couldn't fuck my wife.

I bit back the desire to ask the doctor if they'd actually seen my wife. I watch guests at Sweet Caroline's fawn over her and her ass-length red hair. Kimber can not say a damned word and they're swallowing their tongues, sputtering to get their drink orders out.

That's why I sit my ass on this barstool one night a week when either Aidy or Morgan babysit. Some of it is a throwback to before Kimber and I got married. I like being wherever my wife is. Always have. Some of it is pride; reminding men they can look but not touch. She's mine. A lot of it? Well, I'm confident enough in myself to understand my wife flirts for tips and there's an entertainment factor to their bumbling. Which, believe you me, is a helluva lot better than watching my wife taking her clothes off for singles.

Been there. Done that. Got the t-shirt. It's oversized.

Comes all the way to her knees when I pull it over her.

Kidding.

My wife's conscientious about what she wears. You can be sexy and classy. Exude appeal and still keep all the parts covered that the men here are here to see exposed. She's got great arms from lifting O. Great legs from—I'm not sure where, but damn. An ass I love to grab. And her tits curve on full display through the stretchy fabric even though the collar on her current shirt goes all the way up to her neck.

The regulars here know she's mine. Newcomers croak a none-too-subtle "oh crap" when they get a little too up-close and personal and are told who I am. There's a level of power I enjoy. Because yeah, push the boundaries, touch what's mine, and I'll make sure your next shot is the blood pouring down the back of your throat when I break your nose. And for as much as I'm gunning for Jake at this moment, he's not going to let you back into his establishment either.

My favorite jackhole has been avoiding me for a week. Ballentine knows what I want to talk about; Rex-fucking-Stanton. If Jake bails on showing up tonight I may murder him.

Tallulah whines at my side. Her paw coming up to bat her ear. The bass from the sound system is loud. I'm the jerk that put the distress on her face. She's out of sorts in a new environment, plus I got her these doggy ear muffs off the internet. She looks like a canine *Princess Leia.* I'm sure she'll get used to them after wearing them a few times. I don't intend to bring her to Sweet Caroline's all the time. However, I'd planned on her tagging along when it was noisy, so she wasn't spooked by the changes in the club between dawn and dusk.

The building is fairly empty for a weeknight and everyone and their brother has come up to meet her since we got here, so that's good.

Kimber ducks down behind the bar. I think she's cleaning something, but then I see her adjusting Tallulah's earmuffs. She grabs the pup's snout and places a tender kiss on her nose, pointing to a silver bowl of water she's placed on the floor. Tallulah kisses Kimber back and dives in.

When she stands, my wife grabs onto the countertop. My hand comes to rest over hers.

"What's going on, My Love."

"I stood up too fast and got the spins. I'll be fine."

"Need to sit?"

"It's not that bad. I'll have my bearings in a sec."

We're in the dreaded two-week wait for Kimber's blood draw to see if the last insemination was successful. Because I made love to my wife, I'm pretty certain when I got the pleasure of jizzing in the plastic cup with the orange lid a day later our chances went down the toilet.

It's making this round easier than the last. Our hopes aren't up the way they were in the beginning. It's not like Kimber ever stood on her head trying to help my boys get to where they're supposed to go. However, the fucking the past few days has been less mechanical and we needed sex to be fun again instead of one more "did we make a baby" moment.

Kimber goes back to serving. There's a guy a few seats down I don't recognize.

"The blonde girl with the funny clothes." He begins as Kimber squirts tonic into his drink. "She still work here?"

"Holly? Yes. It's her night off."

"When's she back?"

"Later this week." Kimber is intentionally vague. Partially because the guy might bring repeat business until he sees Holly. Yet, the girls are protective of one another too. There's a policy not to give out anyone's schedule in case of creepsters.

"What's she do around here? The website says she's a manager. Does she dance at all?"

"I'm the manager. Holly's the assistant manager. Neither of us dances, nor does the waitstaff," she replies, emphatic.

"You have those, uh, cubbies, closets?" He gestures to the curtains where the dancers give private shows.

"Do you have a point?"

"What are those for?"

My wife huffs and raises her brow, memorizing the man's appearance. Khakis, pilled polo shirt, salt and pepper hair. I note he has no southern accent, which is common for the Raleigh suburbs, even Brighton.

"Not for you. Are you here for the drink or the entertainment?"

"The drink."

"Want to cash out?"

He lifts his ass to retrieve his wallet and my wife runs his card, returning the slip for him to sign.

"Have a great night," she's polite but clipped. It's easy to tell when Kimber gets a bad vibe.

The guy takes the signal and his cocktail to find a seat near the stage while he drinks it.

Her lips twist and she looks at me. "Something's off. I'm going to talk to the bouncer and security in case that one turns into a stalker or some shit." Exasperation radiates off of her.

I wiggle my fingers in a gimme motion toward the thick stack of receipts. She plucks the top one from the spike, giving it to me as she scoots past Tallulah.

"I got you covered. Take your time." I've been known to serve a time or two when things get hectic.

The first thing I see on the man's slip is his name is William Mayer. I'm in immediate agreement with Kimber's assessment of *or some shit*. When we were naming Owen, Holly made mention that Bhodi's father flipped when he wasn't a junior. William wanted his namesake a Will or a Billy and Holly wouldn't abide by it after he'd done her dirty. She didn't even give the kid his father's last name. So Bhodi it was and the name suits the boy.

I use my camera phone to take a snapshot of the paper and make another hole in the center, putting it back for the sales to be tabbed at closing. Then I punch what information I can into my cell and—

"Viola!" Ballentine's at my side, his arms held wide like he's fucking Houdini, and has pulled a reappearing trick.

"Are you drunk?"

"No." Jake's shit-eating grin dissolves.

"Stoned?"

"No." He gets more serious. He actually thought he was going to get out of this showing up and acting coy.

"Good. We've got to talk." I march toward the office. Tallulah follows her leash dragging on the floor. Halfway there, I grab Kimber by the waist and plant one on her. It's for everyone's benefit. The customers, William, Jake—who fucking needs the reminder that she's mine—and me. Since I do too. It bolsters my next move.

I take Jake's chair, putting my feet up the way he would. My dog makes herself comfortable on the leather couch and I give her the command to stay. Things are about to get heated.

"What's up?" he tries to knock my shoes down, but I won't budge.

"What did you do to Stanton?"

Jake's taken aback. "I didn't do anything to the man. It was an unfortunate turn of events."

My feet slam to the floor and I get in Jake's face. "Rex Stanton had a stroke on the back nine right after you threatened him."

"Like I said, unfortunate turn. They aren't related." He raises his palms. There's a slight tick in the vein at his throat. Jake's not sweating. But the bags under his eyes are the assurance I need that he's examined his own guilt and prove he's pondered his culpability. He doesn't want to admit that to me.

Asshole and avoidance start with A.

"The man is basically brain-dead. Have you thought about how this could screw up Holly's life?"

"Screw it up how? Big deal. Stanton is in a coma."

"Cass is in charge of the dealerships. You know, the big brother that Bhodi hit it off with. How can you be so damn self-absorbed that you don't consider, above and beyond Cary Cass being upset that his father is in the hospital, that he might pull out of the mentorship program? Holly is a good mother. She works her ass off for you and she's trying to give her kid the stability Bhodi needs." I've started poking Jake in the chest. His eyes bug out each time I do because the last thing Jake's used to is me losing my temper.

"What if Cass doesn't have time for Bhodi anymore, Jake?"

"There will be someone else."

"Like Bhodi's deadbeat dad? Why don't we go ask him? He's sitting in the theatre right now. And he was real curious about what Holly is up to."

"What? How the hell?" Jake turns in a circle. He wants to grab the handle, barge down the hall, and throw that asshat out on his ear. But that's not keeping the upper hand or how we do business in this office.

"Yeah, what? Like what the hell do you do to protect them now that you've fucked with their lives? Was the payout from Stanton worth it in the end? Cause I'm telling you, for me, it wasn't. I'm finished. You can take a flying leap if you ever ask me to go fishing for you again."

The information about Cass was a favor to Holly that blew up when Jake saw an opportunity to cash in.

I see the flash of remorse.

"Did you ever make good on it? Do you even know what Stanton is hiding?"

"No."

"And you never will now. You're a mess. You're an embarrassment to the women you fall in love with." I lay on the line what I've always known. "Tell me, Jake, if you don't answer to Kimber when you ask me to do this shit, and you're sending Holly on a ride up shit creek without a paddle, what made you ever think that *she* was the one for you? Her husband gave up *everything* for her." I sneer, poking the sleeping beast.

Jake throws an expected punch. I block it and shove him back.

"We're done." I should have told him this years ago. I wanted to tell him when Kimber announced we were going to have another baby. But if my wife and I aren't getting a second chance, I'm taking the one we did get.

I grab Tallulah's leash and reach for the doorknob.

"What about Holly?" Pussy whipped by three women he'll never take to bed, Jake sounds defeated.

"Leave the Stanton's alone. What I find on William Mayer, I'll share with her… When Holly asks for help."

Music filters from the theater towards the office. Tallulah and I are in the hall when Jake speaks again, taunting to get in the last word.

"Your boo-hoo, I'm a whiner dog looks idiotic with that thing on its head." He rubs by his eyes,

I spin and stare Jake down. "Man, I have a dog, a kid, Morgan, Aidy, and wife smart enough to know that if she'd have fucked you she'd have caught crabs. Maybe you should stop being such a miserable cuss and build an actual life for yourself instead of destroying them."

Chapter Seven

Kimber

"Oh gosh," I say, grabbing my forehead. I reach for the soda gun and fill a glass with a mouthful of syrupy cola.

"What's going on, My Love?"

"It's nothing. I'm dehydrated or have low blood sugar or something." After tossing the soda down, I squeeze my eyes shut and shake my head. It throws off my equilibrium, making it worse.

It's fifteen minutes until close. A few hours ago, Jake stormed out without a word. Not that it's a new occurrence.

Trig's been in his spot at the bar since. His demeanor, a combination of normal Trig relaxed and unbothered, is at odds with the increased jerky movements he's been making in his sleep. It's almost like he's waiting for the other shoe to drop. I won't ask. Trig's business with Jake is not my business.

I also won't cop to feeling like I was going to pass out while he disappeared into the office. I don't want my husband any more agitated. Plus, my boobs hurt like hell and I've been cranky at more people than the customer who asked about Holly. Although that douche canoe seriously didn't help my current bad mood, and deserves full credit for making me feel worse.

This is a raging case of PMS brought on by way too many fucking hormones. I can't wait for next month when I'm not a human pin cushion and feel like myself for more than a few minutes at a time. I'm wondering if all the drugs will mess up my system and a little worried that a side effect is that it'll make me less interested in amour. This week with Trig's been the most fun we've had in months. We even had to lock Tallulah out of the room once. Poor girl. She was afraid Trig was hurting me when I got a little loud.

I look up and bite my lip. One of the bouncers dragged a dressing room chair out for Tallulah so that she didn't have to lay on the floor all night. She's got a spot at the bar, but the seat is so short that when she sits up, she rests her chin on the lacquer. All I see of our pup is her nose and her doggy ear muffs. It's adorable.

Trig's hand covers mine, drawing my attention away. "I'm worried about you."

"It's no big deal. The stupid drugs are messing with me. My stomach is in knots. I'm not eating. My head is just a little swimmy."

Trig stands up. "I'm going down the block to the gas station."

"For what?"

"A pregnancy test. What else do you think?"

"It's too soon and really, a gas station?" I say with exaggerated *ew*. "If they even have any, those are probably expired."

"I'll check the date. The test says nothing, and I'll treat you to Baked Beans in the morning. Coffee *and* a chocolate croissant."

"You drive a hard bargain." I acquiesce.

Trig knows I've set my beta test day as my official day back on the caffeine wagon. Right now I'd kill for a double espresso just for the kickstart to make it through closing and restocking for tomorrow's crew.

My husband is gone for fifteen minutes.

I never get my consolation prize.

A month later, I'm still caffeine-free, laying on the exam table in my OB's office. I've had enough internal ultrasounds to last a gal a lifetime and turn my head away from the screen while the tech moves the probe, pointing and clicking.

Trig's entranced by the monitor. As I watch him, my cheek draws up, my nose tingles, and my eyes get misty.

We're five and a half weeks out. My HCG levels in my bloodwork the day after taking that silly—expired!—quickie mart test were elevated. I cried and laughed, full of unbridled joy, and then cried some more when the nurse called confirming the lab results. I can't believe this is happening for us. My heart has been in my throat for weeks.

What if this isn't happening? What if we got our hopes up to be dashed?

"My Love," Trig says with urgency.

Chasing his euphoria, my head crinkles the paper over the flat pillow. I fight back tears. There's pressure in my abdomen as squishy blobs focus in and out.

"There they are." A soft voice confirms. "Congratulations, Mom and Dad."

Elbows on the exam table, Trig grabs my hand. He crushes my fingers in his double fist and bows his head as if he's praying. When he looks up, tears are streaming down my face and his.

He wipes mine away while the tech is offering us both tissues.

"You okay, My Love?" His voice is low, rough with emotion. With red-rimmed eyes, Trig snuffles.

"Never better." I hiccup as his lips brush mine.

Trig

"Have you woken up yet?" Byron asks me.

We're outside, leaning against the barn at the training facility, soaking up the spring sunshine. We both have our legs stretched out in front of us and crossed at the knees. There's a six-pack on the grass between us—two empties, two fulls, and each of us have one in our paws.

Byron and I get together every other weekend now so Jovie and Tallulah can have a puppy playdate and blow off some stink in the wide fenced-in area. Tallulah loves the freedom of the dog park. But there's no discounting the bond Jovie and Tallulah share. When they're running like mad with their tongues hanging out of their mouths it is a sight to behold.

Outside of Aidy and Morgan, who we've told for necessary reasons, Byron's the only one who knows Kimber is expecting. She's tired a lot, and weepier than ever with her hormones doing their crazy baby thing. But I don't mind since most of the time it's tears of gratitude, like how much joy there was watching Owen blow out the candles on his cake when he turned three, or being uber-serious while he pretends like he's on the mound, throwing out a pitch.

All things considered, I mean, we do have babies on the way, Kimber's also relaxed, which has allowed my nerves to calm a fraction too. I'm conscious when I touch my wife because I don't want anything to go wrong. Yet, Kimber's all in and we're enjoying pregnancy sex to the fullest the way we had when O was on the way.

"It seems surreal." I tip my bottle to my lips.

Tallulah has retrieved a tennis ball and she drops it by my knee. Her tail wagging, I wait for her to plop her ass down on the ground before whipping it into the air. She's lightning-fast. Adding those few seconds to the game with an intentional fake out throw is something it took playing a few rounds to figure out.

I blow out a deep breath that escapes the side of my mouth.

"What about the nightmares? It's been a few months, are you seeing progress? Is Tallulah helping?" Byron checks in every now and again. Reality is he trained my pup for a purpose and he doesn't want her to fail me.

"She is," I respond with a tip of my chin. The dog is my constant companion. I take her everywhere. At night, if she's not sleeping on the bed, she'll get up on me acting like a weighted blanket when I start jerking in my sleep. "I'm still having dreams," I admit. "They're not as prevalent, but still can't stop them and when I wake up for one it leaves me feeling like I'll always be—"

"Helpless to stop them." My Army buddy supplies. "I get 'em too. Terrifies me when they come out of the clear blue. Do you talk to your shrink about them?"

I lift my shoulders and *meh* him. "Sometimes I do. Sometimes I don't. Haven't had an appointment in long enough, and they're not what they were. I guess I know the root of them, so it makes what my brain is doing more straightforward, but just as messy."

I'm almost certain once we're gotten through this week the lingering first trimester concerns will subside. After that, Kimber will be safe at home, doing what she's supposed to do; baking cookies with O, and our babies in the more proverbial oven.

The only big deal is Jake's reaction when he finds out Kimber is pregnant. To shield her from it happening before we're ready, my ass has been perched on my favorite bar stool. I serve drinks when the bar is slammed, and make sure my wife can make it through her shift without over-exerting herself. So Aidy's taken some of my night duty with Owen and Morgan's been putting in more frequent evening hours with installs for the surveillance company.

I'd asked Kimber if she wanted to call it quits the day of the sonogram. My wife said she needed to stay at work a while longer. Managing Sweet Caroline's was her insurance policy in case there were any complications during the first twelve weeks. I understood her motivation, but damned if I was letting her do it alone.

For once, Jake's avoidance of Sweet Caroline's, and subsequently me since our row, is working to our advantage. He hasn't come to me for help. He's dodged anything whatsoever having to do with Stanton. Although, word is someone put Jake on Cass's radar. Hell, the only time I have seen Ballentine in weeks was when the three of us met: Jake, Carver, and me. We keep tabs on mill girls and Holly's name came up. All he asked was if I had a handle on the William situation. When I said yes, Jake dropped it.

"Knowing is half the battle. I'm here now if you need an ear." Byron offers.

Before Tallulah, Byron and I had grown apart. I wouldn't have shared if my breakfast gave me the shits with him. And, yes, that's the kind of relationship we have in the barracks. No holds barred. Frankly, one of us didn't even have to tell the other if our guts were churning over bad food or a direct order. We just knew.

Spending time with Byron this past year, we've reconnected. I trusted him with my life a long time ago and the issue I have is not going anywhere. It'll stick with me till the day I die and what I'm willing to reveal scratches the surface of my reality since leaving the military.

I'm not one to share other's stories, but I don't know how to explain to Byron without the comparison. "So this kid who is dating Kimber's daughter and lives with us, Morgan. He did some time. For what the legal and probation system considers, he is reformed and he's going on to live the life of a model citizen. But what if another guy made a choice, worse than Morgan's?"

"Like killing a man."

"Indirectly." I shrug. "I mean, let's say he wasn't told by his commanding officer to point and shoot."

There's a scenario burned into both our psyches. Neither of us hesitated pulling the trigger when the order justified those means.

"I get it. For argument's sake."

"The guy's done with that. He's moving on." My hand flies in a wave between us. "But is there a point to his redemption if he goes on to live his best life for decades and he can still be incarcerated? If he still loses everything he's worked for while becoming more of an asset to society than a liability." There's a ton of bullshit to this, but it drives home my main point.

"That's a tough one. I don't have an answer." Byron breathes out and scratches the back of his neck. "One thing I can assure you of."

"What's that?"

"No matter what this guy chooses, if his wife looks anything like yours does, she isn't going to be lonely when he's sporting an orange jumpsuit. You think those come in camo? Or are the long black stripes on the throwback uniforms to help keep you hidden?" Byron can't contain his cheeky grin.

"Asshole," I call him.

"Backatcha, Jerkface... I can't believe I gave my dog

to a criminal," he pshaws, taking another swallow of beer.

"She was never your dog. You got her to train for me," I guffaw.

"Still." Byron's tone is even. "I'm going to need to keep a closer eye on Tallulah now. And I believe it would be in Kimber's best interest if I kept one on her too."

"I will beat you within an inch of your life!" I bellow, belly laughing. "If anyone else said that shit to me, man…"

"Then you would be responsible for murder." He smarts.

"Shit. I would. I so would." I scrub my brow, pulling my fingers down my face in a v to the tip of my chin and my almost grown black beard. "I love her. I don't want my shit catching up with her."

Byron nods as if he understands. "Then one way or another you gotta do what's right for your family and hold out hope that it won't."

"Yeah, I guess you're right." Byron's advice is nothing I haven't placated myself with. Though, hearing it confidently come from someone else is reassuring. "Hey, man, do you like golf?"

"Hell, no. Haven't you ever heard what Mark Twain said? I already have to walk Jovie."

I chuckle. "I've brought Tallulah. Got her a cute little vest that says 'service animal'." She likes riding in the golf cart. "I'll score one for Jovie and I'll teach you the game. It'll be fun."

"While you whoop my ass." Byron plunks his empty into the cardboard box.

"My wife'll cook you dinner." I try to sweeten the deal. Maybe I do like the hustle. "*I'll* cook you dinner and have her invite some of her single friends over."

Not all of my friends are lost causes when it comes to women. The dogs take up a lot of Byron's life. He's still unattached and we aren't getting any younger. I'd like him to have a taste of what I do before it's too late.

"Fine. I'll do it for the meal. I hope these friends are all as gorgeous as Kimber?"

I raise a brow. Nobody is as attractive as my wife. At least to me they aren't. Even when our souls are shattered, we're better together. The thing is, sitting in our bedroom that night, ruddy-faced and letting her sorrows and pain out, was a moment I found Kimber the most beautiful she's ever been.

She had faith I'd be tender with her breaking heart while grappling with the belief that our hope was unraveling. The honesty Kimber had shown allowed me to tie a knot in the rope strong enough to bear both our loads and carry the burden.

"Gorgeous or not, you have to find something inside the other person worth fighting for when you hit a rough patch. Hold on to that thought and you might stand a chance with someone as special as I've got."

Thank you for reading Holding Onto Hope! I hope you loved the continuation of Trig and Kimber's angsty love story as much as I do. Haven't read Trig and Kimber's beginning? Pick up **Splinter of Hope**—a heart-wrenching twist on secret baby romance—now!

Find your next swoon-worthy book boyfriend while you enjoy the following excerpt from Holly and Cary's Reverse Age Gap Romance, **Home Wrecker**…

HOME WRECKER

©2021 Jody Kaye, All Rights Reserved

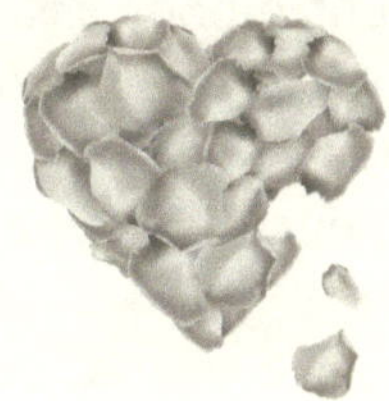

Holly

If there is a God, he smiled on me when Bhodi called from upstairs. Lord knows Cary Cass has an ass you can bounce a quarter off of.

Like a lech, my body leans as Cary turns the corner so I can get a better view watching him leave. I roll my eyes at my lasciviousness. It's not ladylike. How would I feel if my son acted towards a woman the way I just have with that young man?

God, he's so fucking young.

At twenty-five, Cary hides his baby face behind trimmed facial hair. There's not a damn trace of crow's feet around his expressive hazel eyes and his cropped brown hair never gets shaggy, proving his standing appointment with the local barber. It's the kind of perfect a girl would kill to run her fingers through. Not this girl, but *a* girl. One younger than me.

My attention to his appearance is all wrong. Thank fuck I'm not quite old enough to be his mother.

"Moooom!" Speaking of…

"On my way, Bhod!"

I reach for a few of Emory's toys to bring upstairs with me to keep the house tidy. My son and I live in my sister, Laurel's, three-bedroom condo with her and her daughter. It wasn't that either of us wasn't capable on our own. I make decent money assistant managing and from tips tending bar. Laurel and I simply realized combining forces made both our lives easier and cut a few unnecessary expenses; Daycare for her and an overnight sitter for me.

My ten-hour shift at Sweet Caroline's ends in the predawn hours. Laurel's amazing the nights I work. She helps Bhodi with homework and tucks him into bed. She even makes the coffee and gets the kids up and ready before leaving for the day, allowing me a few extra hours of sleep. Then my niece, Emory, and I walk Bhodi to the bus stop and it's my turn to take care of my sister's kiddo.

I'd thought Bhodi would have siblings. I loved every minute of being pregnant with him and couldn't wait to do it again. The joke was on me when William broke my heart. In a sense with Emory, who is four, I've gotten to do all those little things over again that I'll miss out on.

I jog up the steps, ducking my head into the large master Laurel and Emory share. My niece is happy, chatting to the figurines in her pink dollhouse. I stroll into Bhodi's.

"What's up?"

He stands there, all five digits on each hand

emphasize the small brown speck on his shirt. "What do I do?"

"Put it in the laundry?"

"What if it stains?"

"Chill, Bhodi. I'll spray remover on it." I gag when he pulls the tee over his head. Having the olfactory senses of a bloodhound can be a blessing and a curse. "Why don't you shower?" I suggest.

"I don't want to shower."

"Okay, then." My hand rests on my hip. "I have a bit till I have to leave. Let's see what you have to do for math over the weekend."

"I'll shower."

"Good choice."

English was my strong suit. On my last day off, I had to watch a twenty-minute online tutorial on fractions to help with ten minutes of homework. While I want Bhodi to do well, I also wonder how much of what he's learning in school applies in real life once he's grown.

I check one more time on Emory before heading back downstairs. Laurel is breezing into the house.

"Did I miss him?" Laurel places grocery sacks on the counter and smooths her pencil skirt.

I notice the silk scarf she wears tied at her neck is missing and an extra button on her blouse has come undone. I slip it back through the hole and pat the silky fabric at the collar.

"If you need to get laid, there are plenty of clients at-da-cub." My sister has slipped her palm over my mouth, muffling my last words.

"I'm not that desperate."

"Yet," I tease.

I swear since her divorce, Laurel's harder up than I ever was. It has me worried about her because I've been there. In a moment of weakness—after my so-called engagement crumbled—I considered stooping to sleeping with my boss's boss.

Her lips twist and Laurel raises a brow, but we share a laugh.

"Cary is easy on the eyes, and it's nice to have something to look at now that Dusty isn't around as much," Laurel muses.

My best guy friend started dating one of my best girl friends this winter. I'd seen the writing on the walls early on, and where Dusty was the closest thing to a father figure Bhodi had, I put in an application with the big brother program. The coordinator matched my son with Cary Cass of all people. Thankfully, they hit it off during a group outing to a Triple-A baseball stadium for a behind-the-scenes tour before the players reported for spring training.

"At least, tell me you gave him a hug."

"A hug? Why? Oh, crap on a cracker!" Dropping a box of rice I pulled from a reusable sack, I smack my forehead with both hands.

"You forgot. You had one chance to express your condolences—and cop a feel—and you blew it." Her lips twist and her finger waggles in the air. "Bless your silly little heart, what were you thinking letting an opportunity like that pass by?"

Laurel and I dance around one another, placing the groceries in the appropriate spots on shelves and in the fridge.

"I had just woken up from a catnap, and I was doing the same thing I always do; trying not to look. Oh God, Laurel, I must seem like such a—" Laurel makes me defensive. Still not being alert enough to be compassionate toward Cary is distressing.

"Cunt. Bitch. Floozy. Dipstick. Natural blonde instead of the bottle-headed bimbo your friends think you are?" She gives it to me the way only a sister can.

"Hey!" I shove her with a can of beans in my grip.

"I had one chance to live vicariously through you tonight and you blew it."

"I did, didn't I?"

I feel awful. Not only for the fact that my sister sees my pathetic life as enviable, but that I hadn't the common courtesy to offer Cary my condolences for the second time in person.

He'd called last night asking to switch Saturday for Friday. Cary wanted to hang out with Bhodi at the dealership to get his mind off of his dad's death. I hadn't expected he would contact me at all this week, and when he did, the last thing I considered was refusing.

Laurel and I have lost both of our parents, and I remember those emotions keenly. It was hard not to wade through the memories when I saw Mr. Stanton's obituary featured on the news. He'd been a big-to-do business executive in the area long before the Cass-Stanton Group began buying their competition and became a conglomerate. However, Bhodi was so excited to see Cary that he darted outside as soon as Cary pulled up in front of the condo. By the time they got home, it slipped my mind.

Laurel opens her arms and gives me a big hug. "It's okay, sis. When Cary comes to pick up Bhodi next weekend, explain you didn't bring it up because you hadn't wanted to upset him. I mean, you never know how a man is going to react over his own father's funeral."

I let go, closing my eyes. Guilt washes over me and then I'm hit with the scent of bergamot and citrus from the only soap powerful enough to erase the scent of my prepubescent son's pits and stinky sweat socks.

"I'm hungry, Aunt Laurel." He turns to me. Water droplets drip from his sopping hair, wetting his pajama top. "Why are you still here?"

"Oh my God, I'm late!" I grab my purse and Bhodi by the cheeks to plant a fat red kiss on the top of his head. "Later, tater. I love you. Be good. Show Aunt Laurel your homework! I know it's Friday, but go to bed at a decent time!" My instructions get louder as I run for the door.

Thank goodness Sweet Caroline's isn't far from where we live. I'm parking in the club's lot as the two zeros appear after the hour on the dashboard clock.

The early crowd who came for happy hour is leaving the building. The bouncer holds the door open as I slip in. Kimber is double-checking to ensure we're stocked with ice and mixers. Her husband, Trig, has been planted in his favorite spot at the end of the bar for months. His presence doesn't pique my interest until a half an hour later when Jake, the owner, shows up out of the blue.

Sweet Caroline's is a well-oiled machine on evenings Jake isn't around. Kimber's taught me how to stay on his good side. I'm comfortable going to him if there is a problem, but I'd rather not. We're given the autonomy to keep those pesky issues that crop up to a minimum. Jake doesn't like the daily workings of his own business bothering him. He's a bottom-line guy. And by that I mean he cares about how the newest dancer's bottom looks in a g-string and if it draws in a big crowd to make him money.

Trig runs a surveillance company—which came in pretty handy when he offered to find out more about my son's "big brother"—and between the cameras and his permanent butt print in the stool, watching over his wife, I'm certain Jake figures Trig's got everything under control.

"What's up, fucker? I had plans tonight." Jake slaps Trig on the back.

I've already got the tumbler filled with ice for Jake's drink. Kimber takes it from me and is heavy-handed with the shots. Not her norm. Kimber doesn't mind serving, but she's also conscientious when it comes to the staff. Many are recovering addicts and she's the queen of concocting non-alcoholic drinks so they can have an inconspicuous glass in their hand along with everyone else.

"Change of plans. My Love and I need a word with you."

Kimber slides Jake's beverage over the glossy wood.

Jake catches it. His lips flatten a line and his brows pop at the first taste. "Sounds serious."

He turns on his heel toward his office without inviting Trig and Kimber to come along. After he disappears, Trig gets up and Kimber hands me the rag she's used to dry the water spots.

"Everything okay, dearest?" I wrinkle my nose.

"It will be. I saw Morgan at the mill and asked him to drop in to cover for you for a few minutes. When he gets here, come knock on the door."

I'm surprised to hear I need coverage but, "You couldn't pay me enough to waltz into that office without knocking first." The place reeks of leather and sex.

"No kidding." Kimber laughs. She glances up the hall, then back at me and sentimentality replaces glee.

I snag her wrist. "You'd tell me if it was bad." Unless it's an emergency, meetings go down here when audiences aren't around. I prefer it remains that way. I don't have a desire to be complicit in any of the other crap it's rumored the men around here are involved in. Uncertainty keeps freaking Pandora's box locked tight. I have Bhodi to care for.

"I swear it's good, Holly. Really, really, good."

Doubling her adverb sets me at ease and, like Kimber asked, I have Morgan take over after he's squared away behind the register. The guys who work across the street know the ropes around here and are second to none at helping in a pinch.

I rap on the door and wait for Trig to tell me to enter before twisting the handle.

"You can't do this to me!" Jake balks. "You... You bastard. I should go after you like her father on the porch with a shotgun."

"We already have one kid together, so you're a little late," Trig responds sardonically.

"Your pregnant?" My jaw drops and the door snicks shut behind me.

Kimber lifts a finger to her mouth. Besides Jake, I've got to be the first in on the secret. She blushes, and as she moves it away, a second finger pops up making a vee.

It takes me a minute for the silent message to sink in. "You're having twins?"

"I'm getting promoted to full-time mom." She gushes with excitement. "You won't have to put up with my decaffeinated antics too long this time. Congratulations!"

"I'm supposed to be the one saying that!" I give her the biggest hug, adding how excited I am for her.

"You know, just to be a complete ass, my new manager is getting your salary as a bonus on top of hers." Jake barks at Kimber. He grabs my shoulders, pinching me as if I'm a possession Trig can't have.

I'm unsure if the "huh?" of confusion is uttered or imagined until Kimber winks. "Break a leg, Holly. Looks like you are officially in charge of Sweet Caroline's."

Ready to read more?
Home Wrecker is available now!
www.jodykaye.com/homewrecker

Trig and Kimber's original book, Splinter of Hope, was a piece I wrote to flesh out future plot lines. The story *before* the story, so to say.

It had been a while since I'd breathed life into a new set of characters. The original concept for Shattered Hearts of Carolina was set in a rather unscrupulous world. Over the course of a few years, I'd actually gotten amazing feedback on the initial draft chapters of a book that's still a few years away tentatively titled Fractured Life. However, the more research I did, the more I realized that while I love reading dark romance, there were parts of creating a grittier universe that didn't set well with me. In addition, my confidence wavered over how off-putting this new series would be to readers who are enamored with Kingsbrier. I've often said I can't write a book until I'm one-hundred percent in. I can't rush a story, even one I'm desperate to tell (uh, Carver & Sloan, and Jake's past!) I actually have to learn *how* to write it first. But I also was unwilling to leave these characters on the shelf any longer.

After tearing away what I thought I knew about the mill, the plots weren't dynamic enough to play out without a great deal more story setting. Trig and Kimber soon became the glue that held Carver's mill and Sweet Caroline's together. Beyond that, they allowed me to take chances with raw, emotional storylines that I'd never intended to write within this series. (See me learning to write gritty?) When readers immediately connected with Trig and Kimber, I knew this couple had to come back. This second short story for them was on my to-write list for months while I bled out Home Wrecker.

The problem was I only had a single solid idea for Holding Onto Hope in my notes, given to me by Jessie (a world of thanks, girl!) when she beta read Splinter of Hope. Still, there was literally nothing to Holding Onto Hope other than the suggestion that Trig needed an emotional support animal until Home Wrecker went to edits. Tallulah wasn't enough to build an entire storyline around. Then almost overnight I'd found a way to compress every angsty bit that you adore of Trig and Kimber into a book that did them justice.

Holding Onto Hope explains a few nuances of the next book from a different perspective. If you've read the entire series so far, you realize that not everyone has the whole story about everything. For instance, Kimber still doesn't know Aidy and Morgan's underlying connection and that the ugliness of life *has* touched her daughter. Keeping secrets, refusing to betray confidences, and for the most part, a character staying in their lane is sort of a hallmark to making what happens in Brighton work. You'll find Holly has the same mindset dealing with Jake in Home Wrecker.

Thank every one of you who has cheered on this series from the get-go as well as those who found Shattered Hearts over the past year. There are always moments when I wonder if the effort is worthwhile. You have definitely made the hours I've poured into these books rewarding.

Ending on an extremely personal note: For those of you who are or have coped with infertility, I feel your journey in the deepest places of my heart. It was a conscientious choice not to delve too far into fertility diagnosis and treatments. Some wounds you're better off not picking at. My parallels to Kimber's emotions have fifteen years of healing behind them. I won't lie and say hope never wavered. There were times the thread was as frayed as our nerves were. But it taught me to hold on, and that hope isn't a single focused thing, it's learning you have the strength to endure and accepting that you'll make it through, no matter the outcome.

Also by Jody Kaye

Shattered Hearts of Carolina
Splinter of Hope
Shred of Decency
Sliver of Truth
Holding Onto Hope
Home Wrecker
Deep Gap
Bleeding Heart
Shattered Soul

The Kingsbrier Legacy
Love Thy Neighbor
Gray Sin
Going Down

The Kingsbrier Quintuplets
Eric
Brier
Daveigh
Miss Cavanaugh
Cavanaugh
Adam
Colette
Colton

The Canvas Duet
Canvas
Imprint

To view more great titles, sign up for Jody Kaye's newsletter, or find her on social media go to www.jodykaye.com or

Scan Now!

About the Author

Jody's husband asked what she'd been doing all day. After five years she finally confessed, "When no one is around, I write."

Okay, it was more like a bunch of stammering and trying to get out of saying a thing. Jody's a writer. You want it pretty. Let's compromise.

"Just finish one," he said, challenging her to complete a story and share it. Little did he know that those words of encouragement meant they'd return from a family vacation with a wild and defiant set of quintuplets stumbling their way into adulthood. Wasn't raising their three sons enough?

A native of nowhere, Jody settled in New England for 17 years before agreeing to uproot her brood of boys and move to North Carolina. She's a part-time graphic designer and marketeer with over twenty years' experience, and full-time writer. If Jody ever gets lost, you'll find her reading, all the while hoping that her ravenous children haven't eaten all the ingredients before she's cooked dinner.

Add your voice and help readers discover
this love story by writing a review!

www.ingramcontent.com/pod-product-compliance
Lightning Source LLC
Chambersburg PA
CBHW061552310726
48972CB00008B/2724